WHERE DOES ELECTRICITY COME FROM?

Susan Mayes

Designed by Mike Pringle
Illustrated by John Shackell and John Scorey

Series editor: Heather Amery

CONTENTS

Electricity at work

Electricity gives power, light and heat to cities, towns and villages all over the world.

Electricity makes street lights work and powers a high speed train.

It can travel long distances to work in places far away.

You cannot see electricity but you can see where it is working around you, all the time.

How is electricity made? How does it get to your home and what can it do?

You can find out about all of these things in this book.

3

Electricity and light

The first electric light bulb was made by Thomas Edison over 100 years ago, in 1879. Now millions of them are used all over the world.

How many light bulbs can you count in and around your home?

Inside a light bulb

When you turn on a switch, electricity goes through the wires into the bulb.

It goes into a thin coil of wire, called a filament, and makes it heat up.

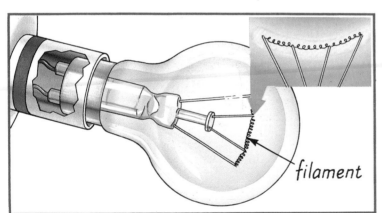

filament

Did you know?

Some lighthouses use lamps which are 20 times brighter than bulbs in your home.

The filament is made of a metal called tungsten, which gets hot without melting.

It gets hotter and hotter until it glows white. This glow is the light you see.

Special mirrors make the light shine as far as 24 miles out across the sea.

Electricity can be very dangerous. Never play with it.

Electricity and heat

Special wires which carry electricity heat up when the electricity flows through them.

Hot wires are very useful because they heat up all sorts of things.

An electric heater has heating wires inside. When electricity goes through them, they get hot and the heater warms the room.

Electricity heats coils of wire in a hairdryer. A fan blows air over the hot wires. This heats up the air so you can dry your hair.

On most electric ranges, each ring has a heating wire inside. The electricity flows through and heats the ring, so you can cook on it.

Did you know?

Some soccer fields have heating wires under the ground.

They stop the field from freezing when the weather is cold.

How a battery works

Some toys need a small amount of electricity to make them work. They get it from a battery.

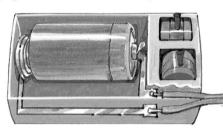

Inside the battery, special chemicals work together to make the electricity. It then travels through the wires to make the toy work. The battery stops working when the chemicals are used up.

Things which use batteries

A digital watch uses electricity from a tiny, thin battery.

A flashlight bulb lights up when electricity from the batteries passes through it.

A car has a special, powerful battery. Its electricity makes the engine, lights and heater work.

Try this

Ask a grown-up to help you try this.
To light up a bulb you will need:
2 pieces of flex – wire covered with plastic
a 1.5 volt flashlight battery, a 1.5 volt
  flashlight bulb and a bulb holder
sticky tape and a small screwdriver
a pair of scissors

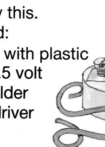

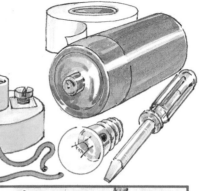

Screw the bulb into the bulb holder.

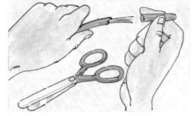

Strip off the plastic at each end of the wire.

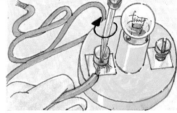

Fix the end of one wire to the bulb holder.

Fix the second piece of wire to the other side of the holder.

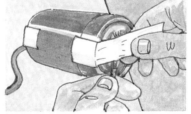

Use sticky tape to fix one piece of wire to each end of the battery.

Watch the bulb light up when the electricity passes through it.

Electricity which moves along a wire is called electric current.

If the current cannot go along its path, or circuit, the light goes off.

How a telephone works

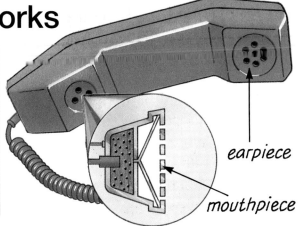

earpiece

mouthpiece

When you dial a number, an electric message goes to the telephone exchange. It tells the machine in the exchange which telephone to ring.

There is a microphone inside the mouthpiece. It changes the sound of your voice into electric signals which can be sent along cables.

Some cables go under the sea to take messages to other countries.

The person you are talking to hears you through the earpiece.

Some cables go overground but most go underground. The signals can travel thousands of miles.

There is a tiny loudspeaker inside the earpiece. It changes the signals back into the sound of your voice.

About television

Electricity makes your television work as soon as you switch on. It brings you the pictures you see and the sounds you hear.

How it works

A television camera turns pictures into electric signals.	The signals travel along a cable to a television transmitter.	The television antenna on your house picks up the signals.

The microphone picks up sounds and turns them into more signals.	It sends the picture and sound signals through the air.	The television turns the signals back into pictures and sounds.

Did you know?

In space, machines called satellites can pick up electrical signals from radios, telephones and televisions. They send them round the world.

The signals are sent by a big transmitter.

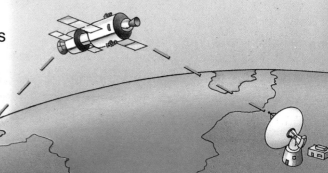

Electricity to your home

Electricity is made in a power station. At the power station it is fed into a transformer.

The transformer makes the electricity stronger so lots of power can be sent to people who need it.

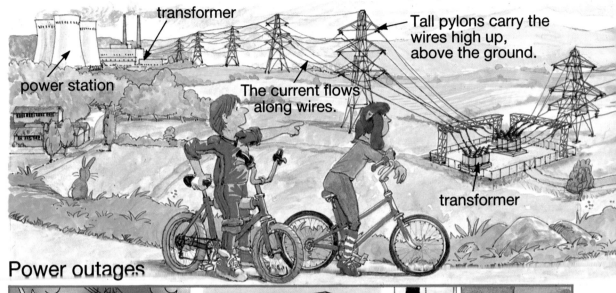

transformer

Tall pylons carry the wires high up, above the ground.

power station

The current flows along wires.

transformer

Power outages

Sometimes, lightning strikes a power line and damages it.

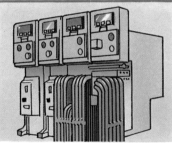

Circuit breakers stop electricity flowing along the broken part.

Some people have no electricity until the line is mended.

Electricity is fed around the country to other transformers. They make it weaker, so you can use it at home.

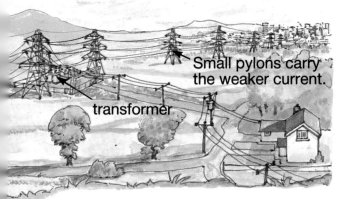

Small pylons carry the weaker current.

transformer

Under the ground
In some towns, electric cables go under the ground. They bring the current into your home.

Workmen often dig up the road to repair the cables underneath.

In the house

The wires which carry power round your house are hidden safely in walls, in ceilings or under floors.

Plugging in
Electricity makes tools, lamps and electrical machines work anywhere you can plug them in.

The plug fits into a socket at the wall. When it is switched on, the electricity goes along the wire.

How electricity is made

The electricity which is used in your home is made in different kinds of power stations.

Using coal and oil

Coal and oil were made millions of years ago, deep inside the Earth. They are used in some power stations to make electricity.

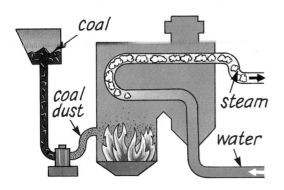

coal

coal dust

steam

water

The coal and oil is burned in a boiler to heat water. When the water gets very hot, it turns into steam.

The steam goes along pipes to a machine called a turbine. It pushes against the metal blades and makes them spin very fast.

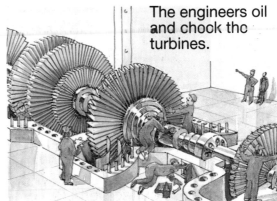

The engineers oil and check the turbines.

As the turbine spins, it works a machine called a generator. This makes the electricity.

Nuclear power stations

Nuclear power stations use fuel called uranium. It is dug out of the ground and used in a special way to make electricity.

The reactor

The uranium is made into rods. Inside the power station, they are put into the reactor. They are used to make heat.

Visitors can stand behind a window to look at the refuelling machine.

Uranium sends out something dangerous which you cannot see, called radiation. A concrete shield round the reactor keeps it safe.

Water and steam

The heat made in the reactor boils water in pipes. This turns into steam which goes to the turbines.

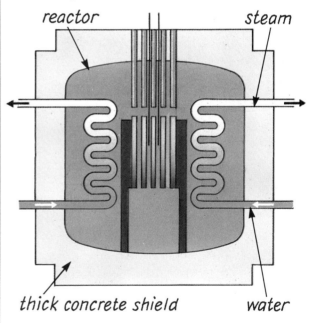

reactor   steam

thick concrete shield   water

The steam spins the turbines. They work the generator, which makes electricity like generators in other power stations.

Power from water

A hydro-electric power station uses falling water to make electricity. The water comes from a huge lake called a reservoir.

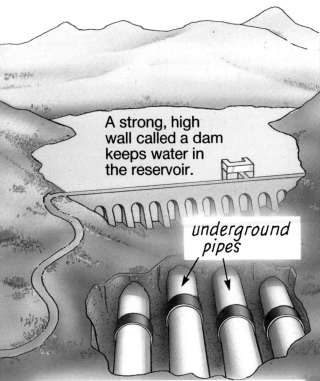

A strong, high wall called a dam keeps water in the reservoir.

underground pipes

The water from the reservoir rushes downhill, through huge pipelines. Some are about 33 feet wide.

The turbines

At the bottom of each pipeline the water works the turbine runner.

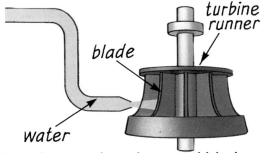

turbine runner

blade

water

It pushes against the metal blades to make the runner turn quickly.

The generator

When the turbine runner spins it works the generator and this makes the electricity.

Saving the water

top reservoir

Streams or rivers flow into the reservoir all the time and keep it full of water.

In hydro-electric power stations the water flows away, after it has been used to make electricity.

lower reservoir

Some power stations save the water and use it again and again.

The water works the turbines, then it runs into a lower reservoir.

The pump

Fishing

Electricity works huge pumps. They push the water back up to the top reservoir, ready to be used again.

The water which has been used in the power station is clean. Fish can live in the reservoir.

Going places

Electricity is used to work high speed trains, subway trains, ships and airplanes. It even works the controls of space rockets.

Electric trains

Electric trains get electricity from overhead wires, or a third rail on the ground. It goes into motors which turn the wheels.

overhead wires

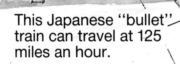

This Japanese "bullet" train can travel at 125 miles an hour.

Tracks and wires

Trollies pick up electric current from overhead wires.

Some trollies pick it up from an electric rail in a slot in the ground.

Subway trains are worked by electricity from extra rails.

On the sea and in the air

Electricity works special controls and instruments on ships and airplanes.

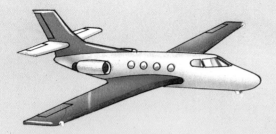

Electric circuits work dials and levers in an airplane.

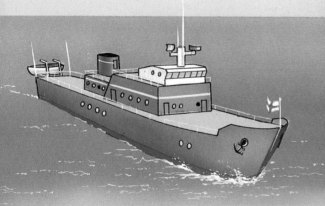

A ship needs electricity to give light and heat. It is also used to work the radio and control the steering.

Space travel

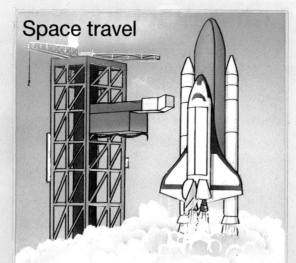

The Space Shuttle is fired into space by electric signals.

Electric circuits in a computer help the crew to fly the Shuttle and work scientific instruments.

17

Other electricity

There is a kind of electricity called static electricity. It does not flow through wires like electric current, but it does some amazing things.

Try this

Rub a plastic pen on a wool sweater for about 30 seconds.

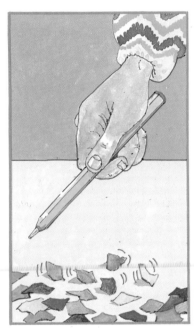

Hold the pen very close to some small pieces of thin paper.

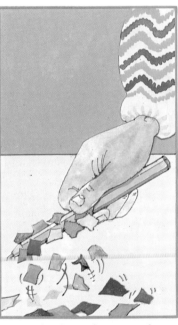

Watch the pieces of paper move towards the pen and stick to it.

Why it works

This works because static electricity builds up in the pen when you rub it against the wool.

It is the static electricity which pulls the paper towards the pen, making it jump, like magic.

Did you know?

Before a thunderstorm, static electricity builds up in storm clouds. When there is too much, it escapes as a flash of lightning.

Tall buildings have a metal strip down the outside, called a lightning conductor.

If lightning strikes a building which has a conductor, it travels through the metal, down to the ground.

Tiny sparks

Lightning hit a tree during a storm in South Dakota, America. Static electricity made the tree light up.

Tiny sparks twinkled on the end of each twig, like fairy lights.

Electricity in fish

An electric eel can make electricity in its body.

It stuns its prey with an electric shock, before eating it.

Power in the future

Using the wind

One day all the coal and oil which help make electrical power will be used up. Scientists are working to find new ways of making electricity.

The wind has powered windmills for hundreds of years. Now it is used to work special windmills which make electric power.

Using the sun

Something called a solar panel can be put into your roof. It traps the sun's heat to warm the house.

Sunlight can make electricity using an invention called a solar cell.

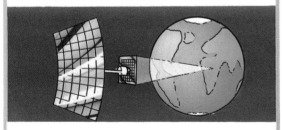

One day, scientists may put a solar collector, made of lots of solar cells, into space. The electricity made would be beamed to Earth.

When the wind blows, it pushes against the huge blades and makes them turn. The moving blades work the generator to make electricity.

Using the waves

Scientists are working out how to get power from the movement of waves, far out at sea. It could make lots of electricity to use on land.

tidal power station

Some countries hope to build tidal power stations. These will make electricity using the flow of the tide, as it goes in and out.

High speed travel

In the future, electric trains may not need wheels. They will hover above special electric tracks.

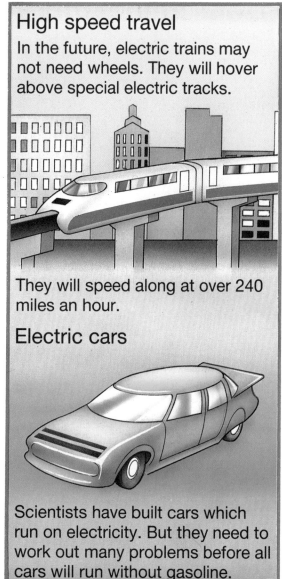

They will speed along at over 240 miles an hour.

Electric cars

Scientists have built cars which run on electricity. But they need to work out many problems before all cars will run without gasoline.

Useful words

You can find all of these words in this book. The pictures will help you to remember what the words mean.

antenna

This picks up electrical signals from the air. If you have a television in your house, or a radio in your car, you need an antenna.

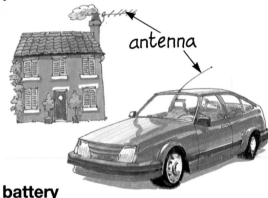

antenna

battery

This has special chemicals inside. They work together to make small amounts of electricity.

cables

These wires carry electric signals under the ground. They have a special covering to protect them.

circuit

An electric circuit is a path of wires. The electricity must travel all the way round to work something electrical.

filament

This is the very thin coil of wire inside a light bulb. When electricity flows through, it glows brightly.

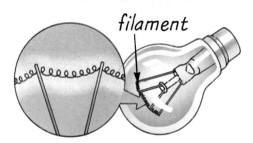

filament

generator

This machine makes electricity. Huge generators make electricity in power stations.

telephone exchange

This is where machines ring the telephone number you have dialled.

pylons

These are strong, steel towers which carry electric wires safely, high above the ground.

transformer

This changes the electricity to make it stronger or weaker.

reactor

This is the part of a nuclear power station where special fuel rods are used to make heat.

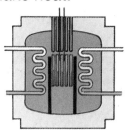

turbine

This is a kind of machine which is worked by water, steam or air, pushing against the blades.

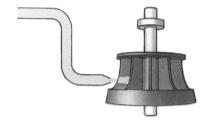

Index

First published in 1989. Usborne Publishing Ltd, 20 Garrick Street, London WC2E 9BJ, England. © Usborne Publishing Ltd. 1989.